Rabén & Sjögren Bokförlag
http://www.raben.se
Translation copyright © 2000 by Rabén & Sjögren
All rights reserved

Originally published in Sweden by Rabén & Sjögren Bokförlag
under the title *Här kommer Pontus!*, text copyright © 1998 by Ann-Sofie Jeppson

Library of Congress catalog card number: 99-052908
Printed in Denmark
First American edition, 2000

ISBN 91-29-64561-1

ANN-SOFIE JEPPSON • Illustrated by CATARINA KRUUSVAL
Translated by Frances Corry

# Here Comes Pontus!

The naughtiest pony in the stables

**FOR SALE**

Breed of pony

**NEW FOREST**
3-year-old gelding
by Black Star, out of Fairy Tale
Good temperament, easy to handle
Forest Stable, Tel: 118 82

Castrated stallion –
calmer, but cannot
sire foals

out of Mom

by Dad

ARENA • *riding area outdoors*

INDOOR ARENA

 Tomorrow I am leaving home!

For several weeks people have been coming and checking my teeth, looking in my ears. Feeling my front legs and telling Sarah to run around the arena with me. They have hummed and muttered and shaken their heads.

But now someone has made up his mind to buy me! I don't know who, because so many people have been here.

"You will be going to a farm close to your brother," said Maria yesterday as she mucked out my stall. I have never met my brother. He left home before I was born. But it was still good to hear that I am going to have relatives nearby. I haven't seen my dad, either. He doesn't live here. Mom went to visit him when Sarah and Maria decided that she should have another foal. That's what Mom told me. She lives in the stall next door. We used to share a stall, but now we just neigh at each other sometimes and play together when we are in the paddock.

"Later on, you will get broken in at your new home," said Sarah. "The girl who broke in your brother will take care of you as well. Your brother has become really good. He has won several ribbons at show-jumping."

MUCK OUT • To clean out the stall, usually with a pitchfork or a spade, removing dirty straw or wood shavings and putting in clean new bedding.

7

Perhaps I, too, will be good at jumping. Last Sunday I jumped over the gate into the paddock and ran back to my stable.

"You're crazy, you glutton," cried Maria when I came rushing in. She thought I had heard her pouring out the pellets from all the way out in the paddock! I hadn't, but I could just feel it somehow . . .

OATS • A feed that gives lots of energy and builds up strength. Used along with hay.

HAY • Grass is the natural food for horses. During the winter months, it has to be in the form of hay.

HAYRACK • A barred rack to put hay in. Fixed to the wall so the horse can't kick the food around and get it dirty. Hay can also be hung in a net.

**PELLETS •** Contain lots of nutritious food shaped into little balls.

**MANGER •** Trough or box affixed to the wall, for concentrated food such as oats and pellets.

**WATER BOWL •** A bowl on the wall, often with a lever that the pony can press with his nose when he is thirsty, so he can get fresh water.

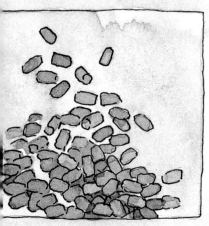

**HALTER** • Leisure wear for the paddock and the stable that makes the pony easier to catch and lead. At the end of the day, the pony is tied into his stall by a rope attached to his halter.

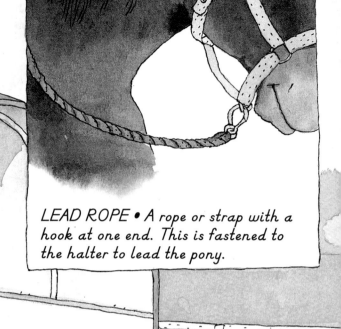

**LEAD ROPE** • A rope or strap with a hook at one end. This is fastened to the halter to lead the pony.

**May 16**

They arrived this morning. A tall, thin dad who ran all around me, pulling and tugging at the lead rope. I couldn't understand where he wanted me to go. "Help!" I thought. "If he is going to go on like this, I don't want to live with them."

"Oh, Dad!" said a little girl with a long yellow mane. "You are making him dizzy."

"Come on, Pontus," she said. "Let's go inside the trailer and have a look around." It was white and smelled new. They had hung a big net full of hay at the far end.

The girl had a little brother. I discovered him too late. Suddenly there he was, standing on the ramp to the trailer, waving a stick. I had got up a good speed to get the hay, so he lost both the stick and his balance. This made the mom annoyed – but not with me, with the boy. She and I will probably get along well . . .

It was very bumpy and unpleasant traveling by trailer. The floor rattled under my hooves, even though I was standing still. And my legs shook for a long while after I got out.

The girl with the yellow mane led me into a stall with nice, clean shavings and a brand-new water bowl. I was so thirsty! I pressed my nose against the lever several times and then went to investigate the manger. Empty!

I was very tired after my journey, and as soon as the girl left I closed my eyes and snoozed for a while. I thought a little about my brother.

Today I took a long walk in the forest. The girl with the yellow mane had been showing her cousin the nice new pony – that was me!

When they got to the stable, the mom called them and the girl with the yellow mane disappeared. In the meantime, I made friends with the cousin. She went to fetch some hay and left the door to the stall open, so I decided to follow her. I walked by the wide-open stable door and breathed in such wonderful forest smells that I decided to take a look outside. I went right through the stable door. Then I heard the girls returning.

Just as I was about to go back inside, I saw the boy. He had a stick in his hand again. I don't like sticks. "Better get away from him," I thought, and walked off in the opposite direction.

May
20

The girls shouted and started walking, too. I sped up into a trot and so did they. Then I took a big step over the broken fence and found myself in the forest. It smelled so wonderful that I stopped and breathed in the air and snorted with pleasure. Just as the girls reached me, I teased them by running back to the fence. This went on for a long time.

In the end, I got tired of this game and trotted back to the stables. As I walked toward the stable door, I heard the rattling sound of pellets hitting the bottom of the manger and rushed straight into my stall. The boy was there, but he wasn't carrying a stick, so I wasn't worried about him. And after all, he had just put pellets into my manger.

WALKING • The slowest pace of a horse, in which the legs move one at a time in a four-beat rhythm. First the right front leg steps forward, followed by the left back, left front, and right back legs.

TROTTING • A faster pace than walking, trotting is a two-beat movement. The right front and left back legs step forward together, then the other pair follow. A well-trained horse can trot very fast.

14

**CANTERING •** A three-beat movement in which the horse starts, for instance, with the right back leg, then left back and right front together, then left front. Unlike the other paces, in which the horse always has at least one hoof on the ground, cantering allows the horse actually to lift off the ground and fly through the air for an instant before repeating the pattern of movements.

**PACING •** A movement typical of Iceland ponies, pacing is a fast, even type of walking that is very comfortable for the rider.

The ordinary paces of a horse are natural movements used by all ponies and horses when moving freely in their paddocks. The rider decides which pace the horse should use.

May
28

A lot happened today. The girl who is going to break
me in came to visit. She seemed very strict and
probably doesn't like mischief. Nor does the farrier.
"Dratted pony!" he shouted. "What a trick!"
    The girl with the yellow mane laughed so hard
she fell over. What a fuss just because I bit off the
blacksmith's back pocket!

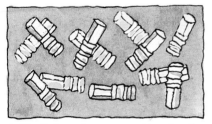

*STUDS • Screws attached to the horseshoes for riding outdoors, to stop the pony from slipping on wet grass or ice.*

*HORSESHOE NAILS • Nails to attach the horseshoe to the hoof.*

*HORSESHOE*

At last I got some peace and quiet and could eat a little. I was thinking about my brother while slowly chewing on a straw. All of a sudden, I had another visitor. The stable cat came creeping in with a kitten in her mouth. She slunk through a broken board and disappeared. Just as quickly, she reappeared without the kitten, but soon she was back with another one. She transported four kittens in all. I tried to peer in through the hole in the broken board, but my eyes are too high up. Then I pushed my nose inside a little – and felt something soft. When I pulled back, one of the kittens followed. Our eyes met for a second, and I realized that I had made a friend for life.

Later that evening, I heard the dad and the boy looking for the kittens. "We can't keep them, you must see that," said the dad. "We have to," said the boy, sobbing.

"I will protect them," I thought.

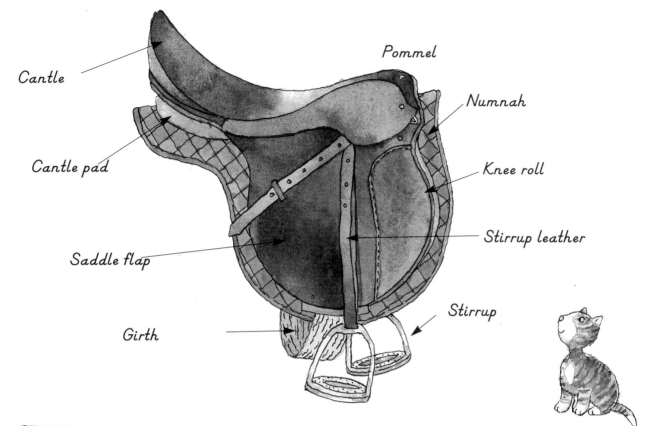

Cantle

Pommel

Numnah

Cantle pad

Knee roll

Saddle flap

Stirrup leather

Girth

Stirrup

June
2

This afternoon the girl with the yellow mane said she had a nice surprise for me. "Come with me to the tack room," she said.

She led me out along the passageway and up to a small gray door. But the door next to that was much more interesting – I could smell pellets through the keyhole! I tried to push that door open.

"Stop it, or you will get too fat," said the girl, just as the gray door opened. What a pity! I peeped into the little tack room instead.

"This saddle is yours," said the girl. "Another pony had it before you, but I have polished it and made it shine like new."

It looked big and heavy. I didn't want to try it on at all, so I backed into the stall.

The girl with the yellow mane was sad – and a little cross. So I let her put it on me. "It fits exactly," she said. But when she tried to fasten the girth around my stomach, it tickled so much that I couldn't stand still. I just had to kick my front legs a little.

Startled, she pulled the whole thing off me and hurried out. She glared at me through the door. "It will probably be some time before she tries that again!" I thought.

This morning I had a scare. A real scare. The girl with the mane and her cousin were playing in the stable. I saw them climbing up the ladder. "I'll soon have some more lovely hay," I thought, and got ready to catch a few wisps. But instead the cousin shouted: "Fire!"

The dad came running. The mom rushed in with buckets of water. Someone screamed: "Get the ponies out!" That was when I got frightened.

I didn't want to go outside while everyone was screaming and carrying on, but the girl with the mane hurried me along. Just as we reached the stable door, a big red truck drove into the yard. It was hooting and flashing and sounded frightening. I refused to take a single step out the door. Instead, I rushed back into the stable. Right back into my stall.

The dad and the girl with the mane had to pull and push me out through the door and toward the forest. They left me all alone in the paddock and disappeared. I tried to jump the fence several times, but it was too high.

I had time to get really hungry before anyone came! It was the mom who at last took me back to my stall. The stables smelled odd, but she said it wasn't dangerous.

CORINNE
1991
e. Magini-
Tamburin

The mom stroked my forelock, offered me a big carrot, and told me that they had been lucky to discover the fire so soon – while it was small and easy to put out. She kissed my nose and said she was sorry I had had such a scare. Her sweater smelled nice and warm, and after eating another big carrot I calmed down.

Just as I was swallowing the end of the carrot, and everything was starting to feel normal again, the kitten showed up. He hadn't heard a thing! "Had a catnap," he meowed.

GLOVES • Special riding gloves with rubber grips give a better hold on the reins – and fewer blisters.

HUNT CAP • A protective hat. (Must be an approved type.)

VEST • A heavy garment for extra warmth that will also take the bumps if you fall off.

JODHPURS • Available without leather reinforcement or with leather at the knees (called strappings) or on both knees and the rear (called fully reinforced). The leather makes it easier to get a grip the saddle and not slide around it.

JODHPUR BOOTS • Half boots with heels that keep your foot from slipping in the stirrups. The heel should be at least 1.5 cm.

HELMET • An absolute must for any rider! Must comply with standard rules – this means a strap under the chin, among other things, which should always be fastened.

RIDING BOOTS • Boots with a heel and narrow legs, made from rubber, artificial leather, or leather.

RIDING CROP

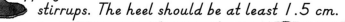

The stable door rattled and the kitten slunk away. The girl with the yellow mane came in. She wanted me to see her new riding clothes. She was wearing new jodhpurs with leather trimming, and shiny jodhpur boots. But I could see that her hunt cap was quite dusty at the back. Her cousin had borrowed a helmet and big riding boots. She looked so dashing I had to neigh. They were going to the gymkhana at the riding school. "We hope there will be games," they shouted, and rushed off.

Where do they find the energy? It is much nicer to snuggle up in the bedding . . .

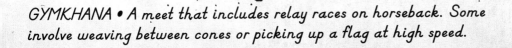

GYMKHANA • A meet that includes relay races on horseback. Some involve weaving between cones or picking up a flag at high speed.

**HOOF PICK** • Used to clean out the hooves so that no dirt or sharp stones remain.

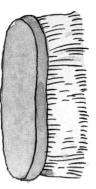

**DANDY BRUSH** • Brushing the horse is a kind of quick basic cleaning of the coat, the mane, and the tail.

**MANE COMB** • Untangles the hair in the mane and the forelock.

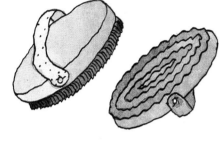

**BODY BRUSH and CURRYCOMB** • The horse should always be groomed in the direction of the hairs. Start at the head and work backwards. The currycomb is used only to clean the dander (the grease and hair from the coat) from the body brush.

KAPTEN GAU
1991

*BRAIDS: Braiding the mane is an intricate job that makes the horse look extra-nice, especially before a competition.*

*BRAIDED TAIL*

June 15

I have been here a whole month. The dad sometimes mutters about the kittens, but no one has guessed what is hidden behind the wall of my stall.

The girl with the mane is often here and takes me for walks and looks after me. Today she brought two school friends home. They wanted to help her groom me and pick out my hooves. The only problem was that no one had told them how ticklish I am – particularly on my stomach. In the end I couldn't stand it and started to jump. They ran out of the box crying, and shouted: "He reared up!" What cowards! And they had promised to braid my tail!

Almost every evening, the mom comes into my stall and stands close to me. She scratches my mane and talks in a warm, soft voice about how handsome I am. This evening she said, just before leaving: "Tomorrow you will be going out into the paddock for the summer. You will be alone there for a while, but you may see your brother. He is in the paddock next door."

It was difficult to sleep after hearing that. What if he thinks I'm just a squirt! What if he gets mad and kicks me with his hind legs? And what if I get left alone in the paddock for a long time?

I pushed my nose toward the broken plank and snorted, and my little friend the kitten came out. What luck! I needed someone to talk to, someone who understands me.

This morning I got really worried. The whole family came to the stall while the kittens were outside. "There they are," shouted the boy. "Look how pretty they are!" I was tramping around nervously. "You'll have to find new homes for them," said the dad. "But we can keep this little guy," he suddenly said, and picked up my friend. "Pontus might want a companion!" I could relax again. What good way to start the day!

The girl with the yellow mane put the harness on me and hooked on the lead rope. Then she led me out into the yard. I hadn't been out in that direction since my first day on the farm, and when I spotted the trailer I became worried and confused. They had promised that I could go into the paddock, but she was walking toward the trailer! I felt so sad and distressed that I shook my head wildly. The girl with the yellow mane lost her grip, fell over, and I was free.

Behind the house I caught a glimpse of a green meadow. I rushed toward it, running along the fence and galloping through the open gate.

**FLY MASK •** A fringe or net that is attached to the harness and covers much of the horse's head. It is made of leather, plastic, or yarn, and keeps flies away from the horse's eyes while it is outside.

The whole family ran after me. I heard a bang behind me, and when I turned around, it was the dad slamming the gate shut.

"But, Pontus, why are you in such a hurry?" said the mom. She had some pellets in her hand and held them out to me. But I wasn't going to fall for that old trick.

Then I saw the girl coming toward me with a bunch of carrots. Her face was streaked with brown and her trousers were torn at both knees. I felt sorry for her – and I couldn't resist the carrots. I allowed her to undo the lead rope, kiss me on the nose, and put on a fly mask over my eyes. Now I was ready for the paddock!

27

I took a few steps. Then suddenly my body twitched. I rolled. I kicked the air. I neighed and ducked and took off across the field, many, many times. For several hours I investigated the paddock and nibbled at many different types of grass.

**ARABIAN** • A purebred horse that is often regarded as the origin of all breeds of horses. Many considered it the most beautiful horse in the world. Keeps its tail high, has stamina and a good temperament.

**MUSTANG** • Protected American wild horse. Descended from the horses brought to America by the Spanish in the sixteenth century. Very strong and fast.

Late in the afternoon, I remembered my brother. I trotted up the slope toward the next paddock and looked over the fence. There he was! I realized immediately it had to be him. He was as handsome as a mustang. He held his tail high in the air like an Arabian. I felt a little shy at first. Then I saw the look in his eyes. The same mischief and joy as in the kitten's.

"Another friend," I said to myself. "This time, one who is family as well." We nodded a few times to each other. Our noses met in a greeting, and I suddenly felt quite at home on the farm.

# INDEX

Arabian 29
Arena 6

Body brush 24
Braided tail 25
Braids 25
By (pedigree) 5

Cantering 15
Cantle 19
Cantle pad 19
Currycomb 24

Dandy brush 24

Fly mask 27

Gelding 5
Girth 19
Gloves 22
Gymkhana 23

Halter 10
Hay 8
Hayrack 8
Helmet 22
Hoof pick 24
Horseshoe 17
Horseshoe nails 17
Hunt cap 22

Indoor arena 6

Jodhpur boots 22
Jodhpurs 22

Knee roll 19

Lead rope 10

Mane comb 24
Manger 9
Muck out 7
Mustang 29

New Forest 5
Numnah 19

Oats 8
Out of (pedigree) 5

Pacing 15
Pellets 9
Pommel 19
Prize ribbons 7

Riding boots 22
Riding crop 22

Saddle flap 19
Saddle girth 19
Stirrup 19
Stirrup leather 19
Studs 17

Tail braid 25
Trotting 14

Vest 22

Walking 14
Water bowl 9